From a life of slavery to

Dragon
Treasure

Stolen from her people and her owners, Lis-Orna learns dragons define "treasure" very differently than humans. She risks her life to rescue her sister from slavery, only to learn that her former owners march to attack the dragons.

Also by F.I. Goldhaber:

Fiction:

Ticket to Faerie

Stranger Than Fiction

Rebellion

Evolution

Firestone

Chasing Time

Destiny

To Rise Again

Finding Magic

Poetry:

Subversive Verse

Pairs of Poems

After more than three decades, storyteller and poet F.I. Goldhaber continues writing professionally. As a reporter, editor, business writer, and marketing communications consultant, she produced words for newspapers, corporations, governments, and non-profits in five states.

She wins awards for her fiction and poetry. Preditors & Editors readers poll ranked her second poetry collection, *Pairs of Poems,* third internationally. Various organizations honor her erotica works. Her short stories, novelettes, poems, news stories, feature articles, essays, editorial columns, and reviews appear in magazines, ezines, newspapers, calendars, and anthologies. She also published five erotica novels under another name.

In addition to paper, electronic, and audio publications, F.I. shares her words at events in Salem, Keizer, Portland, Seattle and on the radio. She appeared at venues such as Wordstock, Oregon Literary Review, bookstores, libraries, and Chemeketa Community College; gives presentations on subjects as diverse as marketing, writing erotica, and building volunteer organizations; and taught Introduction to Indie Publishing at Portland Community College and as a weekend intensive.

http://goldhaber.net/

From a life of slavery to

Dragon Treasure

F.I. Goldhaber

Dragon Treasure

Fantastic Worlds Publishing

ISBN: 978-1-937839-21-5

Copyright © 2014 by F.I. Goldhaber

Fantastic Worlds Publishing
http://fantasticworldspublishing.com
P.O. Box 80766
Portland OR 97280

Dragon Treasure

By F.I. Goldhaber

The dark shadow floated over Lis-Or-na and she looked up to see a long, winged silhouette blocking the sun. She screamed and ran, dropping the heavy water-skin that weighed her down. Kicking up dust, she darted across the red dirt and scooped up her little sister.

Obsidian-like talons closed around Lis-Or-na's waist. With a wail, she let Lis-Anta slip from her grasp then cried out in pain. The frightened child had bitten her hand.

Although Lis-Orna twisted and tried to slip free, her feet just kicked air. The ground receded so quickly her stomach seemed to stay with the howling child. Sobbing, she shoved at the three talons that crossed under her breasts, but her damp hands slipped off the slick surface. She could feel the scales of the dragon's chest pressing into her back through the thin fabric of her aropo. The monstrous wings pushed hot air past her tear-streaked face. The slow rhythmic beating echoed in her ears and countered the frantic pounding of her heart. Below, she could see the adobe hovels of the slave quarters that ringed the red sandstone walls of the city. From the fields and the work buildings, other Owejo shouted at the dragon, shaking their fists, waving hoes and shovels in frustration. Lis-Orna reached out to them, but no one could save her. Someone picked up her sister. From this distance, Lis-Orna couldn't see who.

"Please take her to Ina-Stoza!" she shouted, but no one would hear her words. The dragon had carried Lis-Orna too high. She couldn't even tell if Lis-Anta had stopped screaming.

Ina-Stoza had watched over the sisters since their parents had died. No one else would make sure Lis-Anta didn't starve. But the old woman couldn't help Lis-Orna. Squirming, she twisted again. If she broke free she would fall to her death — better that than becoming a dragon's dinner.

"Do not struggle so, Little One," the dragon

hissed in the language of the Mati. Its paw tilted, bringing Lis-Orna upright so her feet pointed straight down. "I'll not harm you."

Startled to hear the beast speak, she looked along the palm-sized scales above her to a green head, taller than she, encircled by a ring of bony protrusions. The dragon had purple and blue horns longer than her arms and a blue tongue thick as her thigh. Six of its teeth could pierce her body through and rows of others were the length of her hand.

"I will add you to my treasure. A dragon always protects her treasure."

The dragon's words confused Lis-Orna. "You'll turn me into gold?"

An eerie sound emerged from the dragon's mouth along with a wisp of flame. "Gold isn't treasure, Little One. Dragons eat gold."

Lis-Orna could no longer see the city. The mountains that edged the far-away boundary of the plains became more than shadowy heights; she could see jagged peaks, covered in snow despite the drought that had plagued the Mati land for years.

"I don't want to be treasure!" Lis-Orna shouted in the Owejo language. She only knew enough Mati to understand the orders that issued from the city and, when necessary, ask simple questions. "I want to go home," she added in Mati.

"Home to your Mati owners, or home to the land of your ancestors?" The dragon lifted Lis-

Orna closer to its head. "No one whips my treasures with the hide of cattle, and the maize they eat doesn't need slaves to water it."

Lis-Orna stared at the bulging eye, as big as her head and the color of fire and freshly spilled blood. "I do not understand what you mean," she whispered.

"You will, Little One." It lowered its talons, pressing her against its chest again. Now the only thing she could see of its head was the narrow purple beard that bristled along its chin from the bottom of its mouth to its orange-hued throat. "You will."

Lis-Orna hung limp in the dragon's talons, the strength to struggle drained from her like the water from the dry bed of the Yortin River. The air grew colder as they approached the mountains and she shivered. Tears trickled down her cheek and brought the taste of iron dust into her mouth. The pace of the dragon's wingbeat quickened and they rose even higher.

"I will cross over fast as I can." The dragon's words seemed distant and Lis-Orna felt consciousness slip away.

Warm tendrils of moisture touched Lis-Orna's face and she opened her eyes to see green everywhere beneath her feet. She took deep gulps of deliciously muggy air to relieve the tightness in her chest. Below her, dense forests gave way to fields planted in maize already taller than her toddling sister. Beyond, she could see expansive pastures where fat cattle and sheep grazed and lay about. The beauty of it all made her weep.

"This is where my treasure lives." The dragon's wings slowed and they drifted downward.

Lis-Orna saw a collection of buildings, covered with thatch roofs, clustered between the fields and the pastures. People gathered in an open space in front of one of the larger ones.

Its wings beating back the air, the dragon stretched out its monstrous hind legs until they touched the ground, then settled into a crouch. It lifted Lis-Orna up to its head. "Hold out your hand, Little One."

Shaking, Lis-Orna lifted her arm and let her palm face the sky.

"This will hurt a bit." The dragon brought its other front paw to Lis-Orna's hand and drew a shape on her palm. The touch of its talon stung like nettles. "This marks you as Tischanach's treasure, Little One, so all will know that I protect you."

Lis-Orna stared at the red mark on her palm, a circle drawn with lines extending past the starting point to create horns on top.

The dragon lowered her to the ground and waited until she stood steady on her feet before it released her from its talons. But when it moved its wings to take flight again, the gusts pushed her to the ground. Two of those who waited near the edge of the clearing approached and reached their hands toward her. Lis-Orna drew back from their offer of help. Although their straw-colored hair curled tight against their heads, they had Mati skin, dark as tree bark. Dragon's teeth protruded from their earlobes and hung on leather thongs around their necks. She pushed herself to her feet and stood with fists clenched against her sides, but knew she couldn't fight so many.

"Welcome to Fiorcha, Tischanach's treasure," the man said in heavily accented Mati. He put one hand on his chest and showed her the palm of his other. The mark of a red triangle had lines extending from each corner. "I am Sorton, one of Keenoranat's treasures."

"And I am Banara," the woman said. "Anasakkort's treasure." The dragon mark on her palm was four lines drawn to intersect with each other in the middle.

"I am called Lis-Orna," she whispered.

"Welcome, Lis-Orna," Banara said. "You were an Owejo slave of the Mati?"

"Yes." Lis-Orna's lower lip trembled. She watched others, mostly men and boys, approaching.

"In Fiorcha, all woman and men are free. No one enslaves us here. We tend the dragons' cattle," Sorton waved a hand toward the pastures beyond the buildings, "in exchange for their protection, but no one owns us."

"Why?" Tears spilled from Lis-Orna's eyes.

"Why did the dragon steal me from my home, my family?"

"We will explain everything, dear." Banara put an arm around Lis-Orna's shoulder. "But first you need a chance to rest and eat." She made a dismissive gesture with her hands toward the gathering men. "You can compete for her attention after she's decided if she wants to stay."

Banara led Lis-Orna to one of the structures at the edge of the clearing. The dark red bricks triggered a memory from more than ten years ago, when she was Lis-Anta's age. It slipped away before she could grasp it. Banara led Lis-Orna through the wood-framed doorway into a room made cozy with woven blankets hanging on the walls and covering the packed dirt of the floor. Additional blankets that had been sewn together and stuffed to plump softness were scattered about. "Here, child, sit down and rest." Banara patted the nearest one. "I'll get you something to eat." She disappeared behind a blanket covering a doorway leading to the rest of the home.

Lis-Orna tentatively lowered herself onto a soft wool cushion, into which Anasakkort's mark was woven in ochre against white. She kept one foot flat on the ground so she could quickly stand again. Moments later Banara returned with a wide wooden bowl that she handed to Lis-Orna. Pieces of a yellow fruit that Lis-Orna didn't recognize filled the bowl and a baked maize cake edged one side. The smell of the fruit aroused her appetite and she popped piece after juicy piece into her mouth, pressing them with her tongue against the roof of her mouth to savor the sweetness. They tasted of honey and peach nectar, flavors she only vaguely recalled from long ago. She relaxed into the softness that surrounded her.

Banara waited until Lis-Orna had emptied the bowl, then spoke in Owejo. "We hope you'll decide to stay in Fiorcha, Lis-Orna." She took one of Lis-Orna's hands in her own, the tree bark color of her skin dark against the ginger-root hue of Lis-Orna's. "But, understand that you have a choice whether or not you do. If you decide to leave after you've seen what life is like here, Tischanach will take you back to the Mati land."

Lis-Orna blinked several times. Now, she remembered. When she was only three or four years old, Mati invaded her village of brick homes nestled in a green river valley. Lis-Orna, together with her parents, and any others that the Mati hadn't killed in the invasion, walked for days with whips lashing at their backs and Mati guard lions growling at their heels. "Would Tischanach take me home to Owejo land?"

"If you wish. But no one lives there any more. Years ago Tiknoron marauders slaughtered those who escaped the Mati."

"So my choice is to serve my kidnapper or return to slavery?" Lis-Orna looked at Banara's broad face, wide nose, and thin lips so unlike her own. But she saw only kindness in the woman's bright green eyes.

"I do not understand the word 'kidnapper.' And you will find serving Tischanach much less onerous than enslavement by the Mati. Our people have always lived in this valley; have always known and served the dragons. We don't raid other villages for food or slaves. We grow enough to eat and, since the dragons protect us, we've no need to build temples."

Lis-Orna remembered the something the dragon said. "Tischanach said dragons eat gold. Why do they need cattle?"

"Dragons eat whatever gold they can scratch out of the mountains." Banara shrugged her shoulders. "For them, it's a treat. They eat beef to survive and they prefer it alive."

"If you have no need for slaves why did Tischanach kidnap ... steal me from the Mati?"

"Last year a strange plague killed off most of our young women. The few men who became ill recovered. It only lasted a few months, but so many women died, we feared our people wouldn't survive. The dragons decided a few months ago to bring slaves here from the Mati in the west and the Tiknoron in the east. We offer them a free life if they become a part of our community and bear children."

"But my sister is all alone." Lis-Orna wept for Lis-Anta. After years of laboring in the Mati's fields, giving much of their meager food allotment to their daughters, her parents had succumbed to the sleep fever that swept through the slave quarters. Her father, Yaban, had made Lis-Orna promise to care for her sister, then only a year and a half, and teach the child the ways he had shown her to defend herself. Ina-Stoza had found room for the girls in her hovel and kept an eye on them. Lis-Orna toiled each day in the fields for the food that kept them both alive while watching to make sure her sister didn't wander off.

"How old is she?" Banara patted Lis-Orna's hand.

"Three."

"Why don't you stay long enough to learn more about us? If you decide to return, Tischanach will take you back to the Mati city. If you choose to join the Fiorchans, you can speak to Tischanach about bringing your sister to live with us as well. She's too young to take as treasure, but dragons value young lives as well as old."

"The dragon can bring my sister here?" Lis-Orna blinked rapidly.

"I would imagine Tischanach could take you back and wait for you to find her."

Lis-Orna wiped underneath her eyes, with the sleeve of her aropo. Although Banara had the same skin color as the Mati, nothing else about her resembled the cruel slave owners the dragon had snatched Lis-Orna from. She could almost remember living in comfort, having enough to eat, and parents who played games and shared stories with their daughter at the end of the day instead of teaching her ways to fight off a Mato. "Tell me more about the Fiorchans, please."

Despite Banara's assurances, Lis-Orna couldn't see tremendous differences between Mati enslavement and dragon servitude. Other former Owejo slaves who had joined the Fiorchan community shared their delight in their new home with Lis-Orna. They didn't convince her, either.

She could choose not to stay in Fiorcha, but she really had nowhere elsc to go. The Fiorchans had plenty to eat, but then drought hadn't plagued their lands since anyone could remember. The rituals required to become a member of the community included forcing dragons' teeth through her earlobes, and Lis-Orna dreaded the pain that would cause.

Still, Lis-Orna had spent the past year hiding from the Mato who would force her to accept their seed and comforting friends who had been ravished by their owners. One Fiorchan promise outweighed every other consideration. If she returned to the Mati city, Lis-Orna did not believe her father's training would allow her to escape her friends' fate forever. Although Fiorchan women were still expected to breed, they chose who fathered their children. And the young Fiorchan men who vied for Lis-Orna's favor promised to build her a brick house of her own where she could raise her children and care for her sister.

Banara and others in the village understood Lis-Orna's desire to return to the Mati to retrieve Lis-Anta, but Tischanach resisted the idea.

"I cannot protect you if you insist on venturing to the Mati city," the dragon repeated each time Lis-Orna found her feeding in the pastures. Banara had warned her against approaching Tischanach while she ate, but the dragons rarely visited Fiorcha except to feast upon the cattle grazing in the fields surrounding the village.

"I mustn't leave Lis-Anta alone with the Mati, Tischanach." Lis-Orna tried to ignore the crunching sound of dragon teeth grinding cow bones. "If you won't help me rescue her, then just take me back and I'll return to my life as a Mati slave." Lis-Orna shuddered.

Tischanach raised her head, blood dripping from her muzzle. "You want to return to the Mati?" She pointed at Lis-Orna's marked hand. "You can't. You're my treasure now."

Lis-Orna sighed. "I don't want to return, Tischanach. But I can't leave my sister there to fend for herself. No one will feed an orphan or take care of her."

The dragon snorted, a fragment of flame emerging at the edge of her nostrils. "I won't give up my treasure."

"You have to take me back if I decide not to stay in Fiorcha."

Tischanach used her tongue to slurp away the blood from around her mouth. "Anasakkort has more treasure than me and she's younger by two turns."

"If you'll help me rescue Lis-Anta, you can keep me as part of your treasure." Lis-Orna closed her eyes. "When Lisa-Anta is old enough, you can mark her as your treasure, too."

Tischanach beat her wings to rise above the field. Cattle scattered, but Tischanach pounced on one, breaking its back.

Lis-Orna ran across the field, through the damp grass, to witness yet another dragon meal. "Either way you'll carry me across the mountains to the Mati city. The only difference is whether or not you'll come back for me and Lis-Anta so you can keep me as your treasure."

The moon had waxed and waned twice and Fiorchan maize towered over Lis-Orna when Tischanach finally carried her back to Mati lands. Lis-Orna had left the woolen garments she now wore with Banara and put her ragged aropo back on. She stayed awake during the trip over the mountains and felt the cold creep into her bones and the dizziness deaden her senses as they skimmed over the snow-crusted peaks. Tischanach set her down among the scrub brush near a bend in the bed of the dry Yortin River. One tree still clung to the parched ground, as tall as the wall of the Mati city, but stunted compared to those that surrounded Fiorcha.

"You take care, Little One. For the next three days, I'll fly to this point at sunset and wait for you to bring your sister. Then I'll carry you both over the mountains where I can protect you." Tischanach nuzzled at her side. "If you don't return in three days, I'll know you decided to stay."

Lis-Orna patted the scales between Tischanach's beak and the shorter horn that protruded between her nostrils. "I hope to be back in only two days, Tischanach."

The dragon opened her wings and beat them against the hot, dry air. Lis-Orna covered her mouth and nose with her sleeve to keep the dust from choking her. While Tischanach soared through the air toward the mountains, Lis-Orna turned for the stone walls she could see in the distance.

After trudging through the dust and heat for the better part of a day, Lis-Orna had emptied her water skin. Sweat and grime covered her. She remembered the community baths in Fiorcha, the drowsy sensation caused by warm water chasing away the evening chill and washing off grit from the day's exertions. Only the wealthiest Mati could indulge in such luxury.

The sun touched the horizon by the time Lis-Orna neared the city, approaching through the arid fields where the maize only reached her knees. She saw several Owejo lined up, waiting to enter the gate. Hoping to avoid the guards, she slipped into the nearest adobe building to search through the slave quarters for Lis-Anta. The hut looked like no one had occupied it for weeks. In every hovel, Lis-Orna discovered the same: no people, no dishes, no furnishings, no food. She rushed to the gate, afraid it would close with her alone on the outside.

"You're coming back from the fields late." One of the guards pulled her aside when she tried to sneak under the iron portcullis. "We should make you service us to atone for your tardiness."

Although Lis-Anta might succeed in defending herself against one guard, even the tricks her father taught her would not prevent two or more from overpowering her. "I'm the property of Tonis," she said. Although Lis-Orna rarely saw her owner and was only one of dozens he possessed, he was the highest ranking Mato she could name.

"Perhaps we should escort you to him, then, and let him know how late his slave has wandered out among the fields." The guard flipped his long, thick braid of straight black hair over his shoulder.

Sweat trickled down between Lis-Orna's breasts and dampened the aropo under her arms. "I would be grateful, if you would. His overseer instructed me to report to him some time ago. If you bring me, he'll think you caused my delay, and direct his anger at you instead of me." She gave the guard the smile that one of her Fiorchan suitors had called enchanting when he brought her a lamb to demonstrate his ability to feed and clothe her children.

The guard swatted at her ankles with a whip, careful not to let the leather strike her skin and leave a mark. "Not this time, slattern, but if it happens again..." He cracked the whip in the air.

Lis-Orna scurried past, saw several Owejo in the streets ahead of her, and hurried to catch up with them. She followed them to the city's edge where a series of blankets had been tacked to the walls and draped across chairs perched on tables that lined the dirt street. Hundreds of Owejo huddled under the canopy with their belongings. The stench of the privies at either end of the makeshift shelter wafted through the area. Lis-Orna crawled through the chaos, looking for a familiar face.

The clanging of the sun temple bell resonated through the city. The Owejo emerged from their shelter and wearily pushed themselves to their feet. Lis-Orna stationed herself where she could watch the Owejo wandering out toward the plaza in the middle of the city. When she saw the old woman who had watched over her and Lis-Anta since their parents' death, Lis-Orna stifled a sob of relief. "Ina-Stoza," she whispered.

The thin woman, her curly grey hair wrapped around her head to frame a lined face twisted with worry, turned. Lis-Orna saw a sleeping Lis-Anta in her arms. A toothless smile replaced the anxious scowl, but Ina-Stoza's dark brown eyes warned that questions could wait until the Mati finished with them.

Ina-Stoza handed Lis-Anta to Lis-Orna. Tears dampened her cheeks when she put her sister's head on her shoulder and wrapped her arms around the girl's small form. Clutching Lis-Anta, she followed Ina-Stoza and her daughter, Ina-Chiko, to join the crowd of Owejo gathered in the plaza. Hundreds of Mati stood on the steps of the temples on either side. The high priest climbed the rungs of the obelisk planted in the center. The chattering in Owejo and Mati stopped when he raised his hands, his white robes shimmering in the fading light.

"My people. I continue to consult with the Sun and the Moon about myths that came alive to plague us. We must honor their demand that we arm ourselves, march to the mountains, and slay the great beast. If we permit it to continue its audacious theft of our property, we will lose face with our gods. But if we slay the beast, the gods will reward us for glorifying them. They promise to show us where in the mountains the dragon hides its legendary treasure: gold and jewels we can use to beautify their temples and enrich the city."

Lis-Orna gasped, and quickly covered her mouth with one hand. Lis-Anta stirred in her sleep, but didn't wake. The Mati muttered among themselves.

"We face a long and dangerous journey. We'll bring slaves to carry the food and water we'll need, for the gods have said we'll find none between here and the mountains." He waved his hands toward the peaks in the distance. "But, we still must train for the journey. Every Mato who marches east must know how to throw spears and shoot arrows to find the dragon's weaknesses."

The Mati raised their fists in the air and chanted the names of their twelve gods. Most of the Owejo just shook their heads and muttered.

"I want to see more of you at dawn for training." The priest waited until the shouted promises died down. "Any who do not survive, will be honored with an eternal seat among the gods, but we should try to kill the dragon without loss of Mati life. Remember, we leave for the mountains at the next full moon."

The priest descended from the obelisk and

the Owejo and Mata drifted away. Four Owejo carried a cask of maize beer on poles into the plaza and the Mato congregated around it. As Ina-Stoza and the younger women tried to leave, one of the Mato grabbed Ina-Chiko and pulled her and several others into the throng. Lis-Orna dodged outstretched hands and clasped her sister against her chest.

She made it back to the shelter and followed Ina-Stoza, who slipped and pushed her way through the gathered Owejo to a spot near the wall. Several thin bedding rolls lay next to each other. Between them were a water skin and a basket holding a few strips of dried meat and some hard pone chunks. Lis-Orna set Lis-Anta down.

"How ever did you survive to return?" Tears streamed down Ina-Stoza's lined face, but she didn't speak of Ina-Chiko.

Lis-Orna turned her head in either direction and put her fingers in front of her mouth. "It's a secret. Don't let any Mati hear you, please."

"Whatever the secret, I'm glad, Child. I thought we'd lost you to that dragon." Ina-Stoza took Lis-Orna's hand and put it to her cheek. "But, it's hard not to let them know our business, now that we must live within the walls. Tonis insisted all his slaves move inside the night after the dragon captured you and then everyone else demanded protection for their slaves, too. The priest started his ranting and these stupid gatherings the next day." She shrugged.

"Your owner is one of his staunchest support-
ers. You were the fourth slave Tonis lost."

Lis-Orna whispered the truth about dragon treasure in Ina-Stoza's ear. The old woman
worked the dried meat in between her gums,
her eyes rolling back. "Why ever did you come
back? They'll take you like they took my Ina-
Chiko."

"I couldn't leave Lis-Anta here with no family and no one to teach her what our parents
taught me." Lis-Orna ran one finger along the
sleeping girl's cheek. "I know you'll watch over
her while you can, but how much longer before
they feed you to the lions?"

"If I knew my Ina-Chiko could find a place
where Mato didn't always molest her and she
had enough food, I wouldn't care what became of me." The old woman shuddered. "Do
you think your beasts can kill all the Mati who
march to the mountains?"

"I would imagine." Lis-Orna thought about
the predicament the priest's plan created for
the dragons. "The Mati expect to encounter one
dragon. I know of half a dozen and there could
be more. The males don't claim treasure and
don't visit Fiorcha except to feed." Lis-Orna
broke off a piece of dry pone and sucked on it.
"But, they'll not know the difference between
Mato and Owejo men. All the races look the
same to them. Any who march to the mountains could die."

Ina-Stoza scratched under her braid. "The

dragons started snatching slaves months ago. They never stole a Mata."

"Mati women never venture outside the city walls." Lis-Orna tilted her head to one side. "They can tell the difference between men and women. What if we convince the Mato to only take women slaves with them?"

"Why ever would they do that?" Ina-Stoza rubbed her chin with one gnarled hand. Her skin had faded with age to the color of sand, and it stood out in the dim light under the blankets.

"I have no idea." Lis-Orna set aside the pone and gnawed on a strip of dried meat. "I'll think of something."

"If you succeed, can all the Owejo women who travel with the Mato find a place among the dragons' treasure?" Ina-Stoza spread out three bedrolls and crawled into one.

Lis-Orna shrugged her shoulders. "I think so. Right now, there are three or four men for every woman old enough to bear children. And, apparently, the dragons compete to see who can accumulate the most treasure." She slipped into one of the bedrolls, pulled Lis-Anta into her warmth, and tried to sleep. But even the heat of the bodies packed around her didn't keep her from shivering under the thin blanket. Her stomach rumbled. The hard pone and dried meat couldn't compare to fresh beef, moist maize cakes, and sweet fruit.

Half the night had passed when Ina-Chiko

crept into the third bedroll. Even in her dreams, Lis-Orna heard her friend weeping. In the morning, she saw the blood on Ina-Chiko's aro-po and the awkward way the girl walked. Then she realized how she could convince the Mato to take women slaves on their march east. She also knew that she needed to do whatever was necessary to protect Lis-Anta.

The next day, she toiled alongside Ina-Chiko and Ina-Stoza in the fields, watering maize plants and pulling the weeds that survived despite the drought. Lis-Anta followed her up and down the rows, too small to carry water, too young to know the difference between weed and corn.

When she returned to the city with the other Owejo, Lis-Orna left Lis-Anta in Ina-Stoza's care and ventured to the plaza in search of a priest. When she entered the temple of the sun, Lis-Orna marveled at the intricate carvings that covered the walls, the gold that gilded the altar, and the giant red stone that sparkled in the center of the icon hanging from the vaulted ceiling.

A priest rushed over and grabbed her arm. "How dare you defile Sortsza's temple, Oweja?" His fingers wrapped the flesh of her upper arm in a bruising grip and he dragged her back toward the entrance.

"I meant no disrespect, Holy One." Lis-Orna tried to remember the Mati words she needed. "I wish to carry food and water for the soldiers who'll kill the dragon that stole away my sister."

His fingers relaxed enough to relieve some of the pain in Lis-Orna's arm. "We won't take women slaves. They're not strong enough."

"Won't you want women to service the soldiers during the long march?"

The priest stopped at entrance to the temple and shoved Lis-Orna toward the steps. "Don't presume to know what Mati want or need."

Lis-Orna stumbled down the steps as the bell calling the Mati and their slaves to the plaza started clanging. When the high priest didn't appear right away, the crowd mumbled restlessly. He finally did climb the obelisk, and Lis-Orna listened to his words while she searched for Ina-Stoza. He mostly repeated what he had said the evening before. But, one change gave Lis-Orna hope that her plan could work.

"We'll have slaves to carry food and water, for the gods have said we'll find none between here and the mountains, and to serve our needs on the journey."

When they left the plaza, Ina-Chiko didn't try to avoid the Mato who reached for her. She just grimaced when he pulled her toward him.

In the shelter of the blankets against the wall, Lis-Orna told Ina-Stoza of her conversation with the priest while the old woman worked a strip of dried meat in her mouth.

"You will explain your plan to the dragons?"

"Of course. But, you must convince Owejo women to leave their families behind and travel with the Mato. If enough women offer to march east, they'll have to leave the men at home to tend the fields. And, I hope, if they believe the women *want* to accompany the soldiers, they'll leave the guard lions behind."

Ina-Stoza shrugged her shoulders. "Those who are Ina-Chiko's age, old enough to have suffered Mato abuse but not yet mothers, will gladly seek an opportunity to escape."

Lis-Orna nodded. "You must tell these women to run when they see the dragons attack the Mato soldiers. Otherwise, they might get burned."

When Ina-Chiko returned to her bed later that night, she wept into her blanket. Lis-Orna reached over and stroked her arm, but Ina-Chiko scooted out of reach.

In the morning, Lis-Orna tied a sling across her chest and Ina-Stoza tucked Lis-Anta into it. Then she grabbed Lis-Orna's arm. "Take Ina-Chiko with you."

Lis-Orna stared at the old woman.

"The Mato won't leave for weeks and you know how those who travel with the Mato will be treated during the journey. Please take my daughter away from this." A tear crept down Ina-Stoza's wrinkled cheek.

"I don't know if Tischanach can carry all three of us across the mountains."

"Why not?" Ina-Stoza tugged at the sling. "Lis-Anta will be safe in here. Can't it carry Ina-Chiko in its other paw?"

Lis-Orna scratched at her head. Before Tischanach had grabbed her up in the fields, she had never washed her hair. It had grown out in long matted locks that crept down her back to her waist. Now after only three days, her scalp felt itchy and grimy, and she longed for the chance to soak clean in the Fiorchan baths. "Maybe Tischanach will appreciate gaining another treasure over Anasakkort."

Ina-Chiko and Lis-Orna left the village with the other Owejo, watering skins on their backs and hoes in their hands. Lis-Anta, who had squirmed and whimpered in the sling, toddled along behind. They watered the scrawny plants, following the rows away from the city, and kept a wary eye on the lion that paced the boundary. The Owejo rarely tried to escape — no one could survive the desert that surrounded the city long enough to reach more hospitable territory. Along with those too old to work in the fields, the Mati fed troublesome slaves to the lions. As a reminder, at least one beast always patrolled the fields where the slaves worked.

When the lion padded out of sight beyond the wall of the city, Lis-Orna dropped her skin and grabbed up Lis-Anta. Ina-Chiko kept hers — they would need the water — and they could hear it slosh about as they ran east. At first Lis-Anta whimpered. But when no dragon swooped down to steal her sister away, the girl giggled and clapped her hands in the rhythm of the pounding footsteps.

They kept up their pace as long as they could, hoping to get far enough away before the guard lion completed his circle around the fields. When they dropped to their knees, gasping for breath, the city was far behind them, its walls seeming somewhat shorter in the dusty haze. Stunted shrubs, most dead and dried up but still clinging to the red dirt, broke up the flat plain.

After long gulps from Ina-Chiko's water skin, they struggled back to their feet. Lis-Orna settled Lis-Anta onto her back in the sling and they continued east, walking as fast as they could. They heard the growl of a lion far behind them and quickened their pace.

Although the growling grew fainter and more distant, Lis-Orna still saw dust clouds behind them when she turned to look over her shoulder. Each time Ina-Chiko complained that her feet hurt or she needed to stop and rest, Lis-Orna softly mimicked the roar of the guard lion when it took down a defiant slave.

Their bare feet left darker red marks in the dirt. The sky behind them blazed deep red as the sun descended below the dusty horizon. Lis-Orna scanned the darkening sky, looking for the silhouette that had once filled her heart with dread. When she saw far away wings beating against the blue-black sky, she realized they hadn't gotten close enough for Tischanach to see them in the dusk. She handed Lis-Anta to Ina-Chiko and ran, shouting the dragon's name.

Tischanach moved silently across the sky. Lis-Orna shouted again, and the dragon tilted her wings and shifted direction. When Tischanach floated to the ground, Lis-Orna leaned over with her palms pressed on her thighs, trying to catch her breath.

"You didn't find your sister, Little One?"

Unable to speak, Lis-Orna pointed in the direction of Ina-Chiko. By the time her heart stopped racing, Ina-Chiko had closed the distance and handed a screeching, sobbing Lis-Anta back to her sister. Ina-Chiko sucked on her hand where the girl had bitten her.

"Shhh, my sweet. This dragon is a friend." Lis-Orna rocked her sister in her arms. Tears streaked the red dust covering the girl's ginger-colored skin and she continued screaming.

Tischanach touched Lis-Anta's cheek with one talon. She hiccoughed and sniffled, but stopped crying.

"What's this?" Tischanach pointed the talon at Ina-Chiko who stood trembling, her arms clasped under her breasts, her fingers clutching at her aropo sleeves.

"My friend. She would like to join the Fiorchans and choose who fathers her children, rather than live as a slave to the Mati."

Tischanach settled on her haunches and drew in a breath. "She smells fertile. That would give me as much treasure as Anasakkort, but I can only carry two across the mountains."

"I'll tie my sister to me with this." Lis-Orna

held up the sling. "Then you only have to carry me and Ina-Chiko."

Fire rumbled deep in the dragon's belly. She pulled at the sling with one talon, then turned to Ina-Chiko. "If I can mark her as mine, I'll carry her back to join the Fiorchans. Hold out your hand, Little One."

After the marking, Lis-Orna held Lis-Anta in the sling across her breasts while Ina-Chiko tied it tightly behind her back. She whispered nonsense words to her sister until the girl cooed back and smiled. Then she stepped closer to Tischanach's paws.

The dragon wrapped talons around each of the Owejo women. Ina-Chiko flinched, but didn't struggle or cry out when the wings beat against the hot, dusty air and the four of them rose into the sky. Her face buried against her sister's chest, Lis-Anta wept and wailed as they flew toward the mountains. The girl didn't stop struggling until they rose into the icy air above the peaks. Then, she slept until Tischanach set them down in Fiorcha.

After the dragon released her, Lis-Orna said: "You've angered the Mati by stealing their slaves. They plan to march against you at the next full moon and take your treasure."

"We have killed Mati before when they came after our treasure." The dragon's eyes flared to a deeper red then returned to the color of blood. "But hatchings will start by then. Dragons won't want to leave their nests."

Lis-Orna closed her eyes and wondered if she had risked her life and that of her sister and friend, for naught. A tear crept through the dust that covered her face. "Won't any of you protect your treasure?"

"I have no eggs to hatch. I'll come to kill Mati invaders."

"They'll bring Owejo slaves with them." Lis-Orna leaned her face against the dragon's scales. "Please don't kill Owejo, Tischanach."

Tischanach let a wisp of flame escape her mouth and Lis-Orna could feel the heat. "If we get close enough to tell Mati from Owejo, Mati spears and arrows can wound us."

"I think I convinced the Mati to only bring women slaves on their journey. Can you tell male from female and still stay clear of Mati weapons?"

Tischanach made the eerie sound that Lis-Orna had learned passed for dragon laughter. "Of course; they smell different."

"Then only kill the men." Lis-Orna rubbed her hand across Tischanach's snout. "You can add the women to your treasure."

"Well done, Little One." The dragon nuzzled its head against her. "I shall have lots of treasure. I will let my lair-mates know."

With three beats of her wings, Tischanach rose from the clearing. Banara and others gathered around the newcomers.

The moon had shone full four days before. Lis-Orna huddled in a cave with Banara and a dozen other Owejo-born Fiorchans. Lis-Orna had reminded Banara of how she had reacted when she arrived in Fiorcha. Banara decided that the slaves traveling with the Mati, who would panic at the sight of dragons, might respond better if approached by women who looked like they did.

Lis-Orna turned the dragon teeth in her earlobes to ease the discomfort and thought about how little putting them there had hurt, especially compared to what Ina-Chiko had endured. After only two days back in the Mati city, Lis-Orna had gained a new appreciation for the comforts of Fiorcha. Daily baths, ample food, adequate space, and soft bedding all seemed luxurious. But to live free of the fear of rape — to know Lis-Anta would grow up never even knowing that fear — gave Lis-Orna's life a new meaning.

Now she had to wonder if the dragons would protect Fiorcha from the Mati. Only three females and half a dozen male dragons watched from the crags above them. Lis-Orna tried to figure out how many Mato had enough years, skill, and strength to follow the high priest east to the mountains and how many Owejo would accompany them. She worried that the priest might have changed his mind about bringing women slaves. Had Ina-Stoza convinced enough Owejo women to travel so that the Mato would leave the men behind?

A shriek that resembled an eagle's cry only to someone who had never heard a dragon laugh startled the women and brought them to their feet. They peered out of the cave entrance, hidden behind a fallen boulder, and saw the dust clouds announcing the arrival of the Mati invaders. Lis-Orna sobbed when she saw the hundreds and hundreds of Mato marching toward them, more than she had ever seen gathered together before. They must have emptied the city. She feared the dragons could never protect them against that many, especially since so few of them had chosen to fight.

She watched the cloud grow larger as the sun rose over the mountains behind them and neared its zenith. The men held spears and bows as tall as themselves. Quivers of arrows on their backs made them look as if they wore feathered headdresses. Owejo slaves trudged along with the soldiers, burdened with packs and water skins. Several pairs of women walked with giant versions of the Mati bows resting on their shoulders. Lis-Orna couldn't see a single lion.

One of the male dragons took to the air. Gleaming black with gold scales striping his sides, he soared over the invaders. Arrows and spears rose out of the dust to greet him, but he stayed higher than they could reach. That height also prevented him from spewing fire across the Mato. His appearance had the desired effect. Dozens of screaming Owejo slaves ran away from the multitudes of soldiers. Their attention focused on the dragon, none of the Mato tried to stop them.

The male dragon rose higher and turned back toward the mountains. Tischanach glided down from the crags. Lis-Orna shivered and her heart missed a beat. The dragon had given Lis-Orna the opportunity to avoid rape and protect her sister. And she, at least, honored the promise made to protect Fiorchans. Lis-Orna hoped the Mato wouldn't injure Tischanach.

The dragon soared over the soldiers, taunting them into sending more arrows and spears into the air. She circled above the Mato time and again, while the projectiles pierced the sky below her. Lis-Orna could hear Tischanach's laughter, but saw no flames.

Some of the soldiers had pointed the giant bows toward the sky. The weapon required three men to fire it — two to hold it and one to use his body weight to pull the string back. Tischanach repeated the eagle shriek and the other dragons leapt from their hiding places and took to the air. They plunged toward the soldiers. When they flew close enough that weapons could reach them, they belched fire. Lis-Orna covered her ears to shut out the Mato screams.

A screech pitched as high as an eagle's cry but louder than a lion's roar reverberated through her bones and sent pain searing through her head. She saw one of the male dragons, one who had gold scales marking circles across his back, tumbling through the air with an arrow from a giant bow piercing his throat and rips in his left wing membranes. She tried to see if Tischanach had suffered any hurt, but the dust kicking up from the battle obscured her view.

Dozens of Mato ran from the flames and headed for the shelter of the caves and craggy rocks. The Fiorchan women took advantage of the rout, emerging from the caves to lope across the battlefield toward the Owejo. Burned bodies littered the ground around them and the stench made breathing difficult. Although she wanted to see the Mato destroyed, Lis-Orna gagged at the sight of the slaughter. Some of the soldiers still lived and they grabbed at her ankles when she passed.

The Owejo women had scattered across the plain and huddled, trembling, in groups of two or three. By the time the Fiorchans rounded up all of the Owejo they could see and calmed their fears, the sun had neared the western horizon. Banara led the women toward the caves, picking up dropped Mato spears along the way and handing them out. "If men wait in the caves, we must fight them. The dragons will come for us there to carry us home, and we don't want Mato interfering."

Lis-Orna took the heavy wooden pole with the sharp metal point affixed to one end and rested it on her shoulder. She didn't know how she could use it — it was too heavy for her to throw and too unwieldy to thrust the point into a Mato. The older Owejo women, those who had fought the Mato when they invaded their home many years ago, braced the spears against their hips with the deadly tips thrust out in front of them. Lis-Orna longed for a smaller, more familiar weapon like the knife her father had stolen from a careless Mato.

Banara sighed with relief when they found no Mato in front of the cave, but Lis-Orna worried. The women hadn't seen any soldiers traveling back west across the plains. Those who had survived might still seek a way across the mountains to invade Fiorcha, in search of the treasure promised by the priest.

No Fiorchans made weapons or trained to use them — they had always depended on the dragons for protection and their herds for meat. Only a few dozen Mato might succeed in enslaving everyone in Fiorcha. After the death of one of their own, the dragons could even abandon their treasure. Dragons lived for hundreds of years. A death caused misery among them all and they would mourn for months.

While Banara explained the relationship between the Fiorchans and the dragons to the Owejo, Lis-Orna watched the darkening sky. Then she heard a scuffling sound from behind Banara, and squinted into the blackness at the mouth of the cave. She tapped three of the other Fiorchans on the shoulder and nodded her head toward the boulder hiding the entrance.

With prodding, she got one to stand on either side, while she moved into the cave with the third. Beyond the overbearing smell of bat guano and rodent dung, the odor of sweat, blood, and burned flesh penetrated Lis-Orna's senses.

Fear closing her throat, she stepped aside, heading back out to alert Banara and find help. A scream pierced the quiet. Mati rushed at her from inside the cave, daggers in their hands. With no time to think, Lis-Orna swung the spear in an arc, cracking open a Mato's head and sending him to the ground in a crumpled heap. Two other women successfully mimicked Lis-Orna's movements.

A third woman missed, swinging her spear in a complete circle, losing her balance and falling to the ground. The soldier jumped onto her and raised his dagger above her head. Lis-Orna grabbed the knife dropped by one of the Mato, but froze, horrified at the thought of plunging it into another person, even a Mato. An older Owejo woman, thrust her spear into the Mato's throat. Blood spurted over all those who stood near, including Lis-Orna.

She held her breath, but no other Mato emerged from the cave. When she heard the rustle of wings, Lis-Orna stepped out to see that several dragons, including Tischanach, had landed outside the cave. Banara pulled the loincloth off one of the fallen Mato, wrapped it around her spear, and asked the nearest dragon to set it on fire. She handed the torch to

Lis-Orna, lifted her spear to her shoulder, and the two checked inside the cave. Lis-Orna only saw two Mato bodies, burns blistering much of their skin. She stumbled back outside and gulped fresh air, trying to erase the memory of the stench inside the cave.

Despite Banara's instructions, many of the Owejo women had screamed and run when the dragons landed in front of the cave. The Owejo-born Fiorchans scattered after them, trying to reassure their sisters that the dragons meant no harm. Lis-Orna dropped her torch, rolled it in the dirt until it ceased burning, and sought out Tischanach. When she approached, the dragon lowered her massive head and Lis-Orna leaned her forehead against the dragon's scales. "I'm sorry about the dragon who died, Tischanach." Tears sprang to Lis-Orna's eyes realizing the Mato could also have killed Tischanach. She had grown fonder of the dragon than she realized.

Tischanach made a sound in her belly that reminded Lis-Orna of a hungry baby's cry.

"Was he one you had mated?"

"I've never mated. I've only lived ninety turns. But, Flipnori was my friend. We hatched the same summer."

Lis-Orna threw her arms against Tischanach's scales, wishing she could rub away the sadness in the dragon's voice and her own memories of burned Mato bodies. She wanted to forget the sound of her spear cracking against the soldier's head and the feel of Mato blood on her skin.

"Come, we must carry you all home," Tischanach said. "With so few of us, it'll take all night."

Dawn colored the tips of the mountains east of the valley when Tischanach set Lis-Orna and an Owejo she didn't know down in the muddy clearing. The rain, which Lis-Orna had learned wouldn't cease until spring, dripped off Tischanach's glistening scales.

"Some of the Mato escaped into the hills." Tischanach's voice had a weary edge. "We couldn't see them in the dark, but we think they're working their way toward the peaks. We must fight them again if they try to invade the village."

"What should we do to prepare for the Mato?"

"That's for us to worry about, Little One." Tischanach pushed her snout against Lis-Orna. "I'll scold the dragons who failed to protect our treasure today. They will all come to stand between the village and the Mato."

"Even though they mourn the loss of Flipnori?"

"We must protect our treasure. We must keep our promise."

A dragon's roar woke Lis-Orna early the next morning. She shoved the dagger taken from the Mato into her belt and ran outside. Dragons sitting on their haunches, wings furled at their backs and fore talons raised, ringed the village. Peering about in the dim light, Lis-Orna saw nothing unusual in the maizefields edging the village. Then, a Mato with spear in hand charged from the maize and Anasakkort belched flames. Lis-Orna heard the Mato scream in agony. She listened to his death cries until she heard feet slogging through mud and brush breaking. Armed men ran through fields to the forest.

The dragons settled down once again in their circle. Lis-Orna found Tischanach. "What about the Mato who escaped?"

"They have nowhere to go. Flipnori's death, and the danger threatening our treasure, shamed every dragon who didn't face the Mato on the other side of the mountains. They put all their eggs together in one nest, left four males behind to keep them warm, and now almost every dragon has taken up posts on the outskirts of the forest. They've promised not to return to their lairs until every Mato on this side of the mountains is food."

Lis-Orna returned to Banara's home. Stepping around the blanket that separated off the room Banara had given her and her sister, she choked. A Mato stood holding up a weeping Lis-Anta with one hand over her mouth and his dagger flat against the girl's throat. The man had burn blisters along one side, and bleeding scratches covered his chest and arms. His eyes had the wild look seen in the cattle when the dragons flew across the fields. Lis-Orna held her hands out from her sides and spoke slowly in Mati. "Please, don't hurt the girl. Tell me what you want and I'll help you."

"I need salve for my burns and a way to get back to the pass without those vicious beasts attacking me."

"They won't care if you have a little girl with you." Lis-Orna tried to keep her voice steady and her breathing regular. "They're only interested in females old enough to breed. If you take *me* with you, they won't attack you for fear of hurting me."

"I'll take you both, then." He pulled Lis-Anta's head back against his chest, his hand muffling her sobs. "Her to keep you in line, and you to keep the dragons away from me."

"I won't help you if you don't let the girl go."

Lis-Anta bit into the fingers covering her mouth and the Mato dropped her. In one movement, Lis-Orna pulled the dagger from her belt, jumped forward, and thrust it into the Mato's chest. He screamed and dropped his own knife, gripping the wound with his hands. Lis-Orna drew back her dagger, plunged it into his belly, pulled it out, and stuck it in again and again, until she felt a hand on her shoulder.

"I think he's dead, Lis-Orna." Banara pulled her away from the corpse and wrapped her arms around her.

Shaking and weeping, Lis-Orna reached for a screaming Lis-Anta. Turning her sister's head away from the body, she rocked the girl in her arms until she calmed down. "You must alert the village to search for other Mato who escaped the dragons." Lis-Orna pulled her dagger out of the Mato's belly. "I think I'll keep this. I'm not willing to rely only on dragons' protection."

Banara nodded. "That's your right as a free woman."

𝕿

Acknowledgements

Many thanks to all those I have learned from through the years, especially the Wordos professional writers workshop and Larry Brooks. Thanks also to those who have freely shared their knowledge online notably Dean Wesley Smith and Kristine Kathryn Rusch. Those who inspired me to pursue writing from an early age include Ruth Wright my fifth and sixth grade teacher at Randolph Elementary School in Huntsville, Alabama, Nancy Travis my freshman English teacher at Clear Creek High School in Texas, and most prominently my parents, Jerry and Bev Goldhaber. Very special thanks to my editor, Laurie Lawhon of Fine Tune Your Words and my beloved husband Joel Goldhaber.